MW01278178

NO WAY OUT

NO WAY OUT

A Novella by
Betty R. Wall

atmosphere press

Copyright © 2021 Betty R. Wall

Published by Atmosphere Press

Cover design by Ronaldo Alves
Author photo by Cloe I. Logan

No part of this book may be reproduced
except in brief quotations and in reviews
without permission from the publisher.

No Way Out
2021, Betty R. Wall

atmospherepress.com

For Steph

"She's in a motel somewhere. Something bad is happening to her. I can't quite make it out." Chris had his fingers on his forehead, eyes closed, face scrunched up. He sat in my living room in a big overstuffed chair, the green and purple floral pattern providing a backdrop to his faded blue jeans and dark brown leather jacket. "Somewhere out near the airport, I think."

"What?" I placed the tea I had just brewed beside him on the floor.

"Some guy is beating the shit out of her," he said.

"Who are you talking about? What's her name?" I asked.

"Angela," he said.

"There are a lot of motels along the airport strip," I said. Images of seedy motels, flashing vacancy signs with the "a's" burnt out, half-empty parking lots with pick-up trucks and rusted station wagons flashed across my mind. And some big guy, with a beard and a pot belly, beating a woman because she won't do what he wants. I squeezed my eyes shut and shook my head; shivers went down my spine.

"What does it look like, the motel?" I asked. "Do you

see any tell-tale colours, numbers, logos or anything like that?"

I pulled out the Yellow Pages and started rifling through until I came to "motels." There were hundreds of them. She could be in any one of those.

"It's stopped now," he said. He shook his head, his long, slightly wavy, chestnut coloured hair falling forward and down around his shoulders. "That was weird." He picked up the cup of tea. "Thanks for this." He took a sip and grinned. "I never drink tea, but it's good."

"Who's Angela?" I asked. A tall, lanky, sexy blonde, I bet. Chris and I were still in the early stages of getting to know one another. I took a breath and started to say something, but held my tongue and waited.

"None of your business," popped out of his mouth.

"Pardon?" I turned to look at him, closing the Yellow Pages. "What was all that about then?"

"None of your business," he said again, a smirk playing on the side of his mouth.

"Um, ok," I said, my stomach in knots. I got up and walked into the kitchen, reached into the fridge, pulled out a bottle of cheap wine and poured myself a glass. My lips puckered as the acidic wine swirled around in my mouth. I swallowed and took another drink.

"Wait a minute," he said, "I'm being a jerk. I get these visions sometimes. They pop up from out of nowhere and I space out for a bit, as these scenes play out. Angela, she's the wife of a guy I ride with sometimes. Sweet thing."

I didn't say anything, but made my way back into the living room. He was still sitting in the big chair, jean-clad legs spread wide apart, feet on tip toes, legs bouncing up and down, legs coming together and spreading apart, almost frantically.

"She's told me some stuff. I think maybe she gets knocked around a bit."

Now I pictured a blonde, lanky Angie with a black eye and a bloody nose, wearing frayed blue-jean shorts and a tank top. And just as quickly, I saw her on the back of a motorcycle, wearing short black boots and a helmet slightly too big for her head, arms tightly wrapped around a big biker dude.

"So, who are these people?" I asked.

"You don't want to know," he said.

"This is just too weird," I said. "I don't think I want to do this."

"Do what?"

"Be involved with someone who doesn't let me in. Who's involved with someone who..."

"Trust me, you don't want to know."

"You're right," I said. "I don't. You can leave now."

The legs stopped bouncing up and down; he got up and headed for the door. "Yeah, ok. You're probably right. I should go. Maybe I'll call ya later," he said.

I didn't say anything. He opened the door, turned, looked at me with his big eyes, now turned a harder shade of green, and walked out the door, closing it softly behind him.

I went into the bathroom, tore off my clothes and threw them onto the floor, and turned on the shower, hot, hot, hot. Stepped in and let the water pour over my head until I thought it would scald my scalp. Then lathered up the shampoo and scrubbed and scrubbed. In the distance, I could hear the telephone ringing and ringing. In the past, I might have jumped out of the shower, grabbed a towel, wrapped it around my body and gone racing down the hallway to grab it, just before it stopped ringing, but not today. Today, I would let it ring. How long could I stay in here anyway? Conditioner, that's what I would do next. A nice big squeeze of conditioner. I could let it sit for a while. Maybe run the tub and sit here for a bit. But then, the water got lukewarm. Maybe it was just my imagination. I turned the tap further and further to the left. There must be hot water left. There must be. And suddenly it got cool and then cold and I shut the water off. And the telephone rang. I let it ring.

The first time I had really noticed him was on a cold, crisp Toronto day in February. I saw him get on his bright orange Yamaha motorbike, glide down the hill, get it started and go for a block or so. Next thing I knew, he was pushing his bike up the hill to do the whole thing all over again. The third time he walked the bike back up the hill, we were walking next to one another.

"What are you doing?" I asked. "Interesting way to get a work out," I said, laughing.

"She's been sitting in the garage for a while and I wanted to get her going – just warming her up, you know," he said.

I smiled. "Good luck with that," I said, and turned to walk into my apartment building.

"So, this is where you live," he said. "I've seen you around when I'm walking my dog."

"Yeah, and now you're walking your bike," I said, grinning.

"We should have dinner sometime," he said.

"How about breakfast?" I said, "After you've finished walking your bike, or another time," I quickly added.

"I've got stuff to do later this morning, but how about tomorrow?" he said.

"Ok. What time?"

"Well, I'm back from work around 8:00."

"In the morning?" I asked.

"Yeah, I work out on a farm near Orangeville, training horses," he said.

"Well, let's say we meet around 9:00, then?" I said.

"Yeah, see you then. I gotta go. This thing is getting heavy," he said, leaning against the bike. "Toodles."

I walked into my building, grinning, feeling giddy. What was he all about? This horse training motorcycle rider.

The next morning, I was beginning to have some doubts. What was I thinking anyway? I didn't know the guy from Adam. Well, it was breakfast, not dinner. I wasn't going to his place. It would be fine.

Just before 9, I started walking north on Avenue Road toward College View. Just past College View, I saw him coming out of one of the driveways, wearing a dark brown leather jacket, jeans and sneakers. "Hi", I said, once I got within earshot. He put up his hand. He was taller than I remembered. And broader. He smelled nice. Clean and earthy all at the same time. Like Mennen Speedstick deodorant and shampoo. His long chestnut hair pulled back. As I was taking him all in, I noticed a couple of grey hairs, curled slightly, at the top of his head, to the side of the part. I wondered how old he was, but didn't ask. I was conscious of my own hair colour, streaked with white, sometimes covered with lowlights, sometimes highlights.

"Where are we going?" I asked.

"I dunno," he said. "Let's just see where our walk takes

us."

"All right," I said, falling into step with him.

We stopped at one pub after another, hoping they served breakfast, but most weren't open at 9:30 in the morning. We finally ended up in the Avenue Road Diner at the corner of Avenue Road and Davenport.

"I'd love a burger, fries and a milkshake," he said to the waitress. I looked at him. "For breakfast?" I said.

"I just got off work," he said, looking at the waitress.

"Gotcha," she said. "No problem. We can do that. For you?" she asked me.

"Two eggs over easy, brown toast and coffee," I said. "Make that well-toasted, ok?"

"Got it," she said.

We were seated at a tiny table next to the window. It felt intimate. No candlelight and wine, but intimate, nonetheless.

"I never knew this place existed," Chris said. "Pretty cool."

"I used to live not far from here," I said. "I haven't been here much, but I used to go to the dessert place on the corner all the time called Just Desserts. Nice vibe, just to hang out and get slices of cake half the size of your plate," I said, laughing, looking at him. His eyes were intense. Big, green, but not quite green. Sort of grey-green with a hint of hazel. They changed with the light and with his mood. He smiled readily. Nice lips. The lower lip protruding slightly from the upper. Perfect nose. A big face, but not unpleasantly so, nicely shaped.

Just then the waitress arrived with our food. "Here you go, eggs, easy-over, brown toast and coffee for you," she said, looking at me "and a burger, fries and a shake for you," she said to Chris.

Our hands nearly touched as we reached for our drinks. I noticed his hands as he lifted the milkshake to his mouth. Dexterous, no rings.

"Do you work late every night?" I asked.

"A few nights a week," he said. "I'm working with a few horses right now. I get there at 3 or 4 in the morning, clean out the stalls, take them out to the paddock, start with lunging, nice and easy. I'm working with one now that's quite wild."

"I don't really know anything about horse training, apart from what I've read in Dick Francis novels," I said, "and what I hear from a friend who owns a race horse or two. It's a pretty exciting and thrilling world, I think. A bit dangerous, too?"

"It can be," he said, chowing down on his burger and grinning. "You've gotta be careful."

"What do you mean?" I asked. Horses and jockeys being drugged or maimed in some way, races being fixed, owners being cheated? Fist fights? These were likely completely false notions and all Dick Francis' fault.

"Just mind what you do, what you say. Don't repeat what you hear."

"You must love it, though, otherwise you wouldn't be doing it," I said.

"Yeah. I love the early morning and the horses. Just the horses and me. There's nothing that can't be resolved. An animal won't hurt you unless it's starving, hunting for food or in danger. It won't hurt you for no good reason. Nature's not like that," he said.

I just nodded. "There must a story behind that," I said.

"People hurt you for no good reason," he said. "People

are malicious, not animals. You respect them, they'll respect you."

"Somebody must have hurt you badly. Done a number on you," I said. "I'm a bit skittish around animals. I just never know how they're going to behave."

"Skittish?" he said grinning. "Huh. Ready to go?"

"Yeah," I said. He pulled out a few crumpled bills and placed them on the table.

"I've got to get back to walk my dog," he said.

"No problem, let's go," I said. It took us about 30 minutes to walk back. The air was crisp. As we approached Davisville, I looked up and saw the iron horse sculptures up on top of the overpass.

"Have you had a close look at those?" I asked.

"No, not really, just from a distance. We could do that on our next walk," he said, smiling, grabbing my hand. "It would be cool to see how they've been done. I've done some horse sculptures myself."

"Really?" I said. "How cool. I'd love to see them sometime."

"And a walk?"

"Yeah," I said, smiling.

We got to my apartment, and he leaned in to kiss me. I breathed in the smell of shampoo and deodorant. I turned my head slightly, and he kissed me on the cheek.

"How about Friday?" he said.

***

The morning following the night of visions, I picked up the telephone to call Chris. After a few rings, someone picked up the phone. A second or two of silence and then,

"Hello?" A gruff woman's voice on the other end of the line. I didn't say anything. "Hello?" she said again. I hung up, heart pounding.

I sat on the edge of the bed, not knowing what to do. Maybe I had misdialed. I picked up the old receipt with Chris's number scribbled on it and dialed, watching every digit.

"Hello?" The same voice.

"Hi," I said. "Could I speak with Chris please?"

"He's not here," she said.

"Any idea when he'll be back?" I asked.

"An hour or so," she said, coughing. "You the girlfriend?"

"Yeah, I guess you could say that."

"And you are...?"

"Angela," she said.

"So, he found you last night, then?" I said.

"Yeah, a fuckin' knight in shining armour, that one," she said. "Ya better hang on to him. He's one of the good ones."

"How did he find you?" I asked.

"Hell if I know. He's got that sixth sense, ya know? He sees stuff."

"You ok?" I asked.

"Better now. He's lettin' me hang here for a couple o' days. I'll tell him you called."

"Thanks," I said and hung up the phone.

A few minutes later, the buzzer went. "Hello?" I said.

"Hey, it's me." I buzzed him in.

He strode in, strands of hair falling out of his ponytail, streaks of dirt on his jeans, hands dirty, shoes muddied. A bit wild-eyed, he pulled me in for a bear hug. I resisted for a moment, then felt myself relax against him, dirty and muddied as he was.

"God, I need a shower," he said. "What a night. I found her, you know."

"Where? How did you find her? Please don't say 'none of your business.'"

"It's probably a good thing you kicked me out last night," he said, shrugging out of his jacket and kicking off his shoes. Dirt oozed out of his sneakers. Once white socks now black. "After I left, I kept seeing a neon sign that looked like one of those cheap motels along the airport strip. Like you said. I've seen her there before. She works in the strip club next door." He paused. "As a waitress."

"She sounds tough," I said.

"What do you mean?"

"Uh, I can't imagine it's easy working in a strip club, even if it's as a waitress. I'm sure there are guys who think they can do whatever they want. That you're there to please them in any capacity they choose. I called your house a little while ago, and she answered the phone. She has a rough sounding voice," I said. "So, what happened?"

"You called my house? And she answered the phone? Huh. I got there, walked into the club and asked one of the bartenders if he'd seen her. He told me her husband had come in, drunk and high. She went on her break and he hadn't seen her since. I walked out the back and there she was, slumped against the brick wall, holding a cocktail napkin up against her left eye. Her nose had stopped bleeding."

"Her husband? He's the guy you ride with sometimes?"

"Yeah, Big Steve."

"What's he gonna do when he finds out she's at your place? Are you nuts?"

"What was I supposed to do? Leave her there? Take her home to her husband? I had to help her." He unbuckled his belt, took off his jeans and pulled the dark green polo shirt over his head. "Do you mind if I take a shower?"

"Look at you – what am I supposed to say 'no?' Go ahead. Here – I'll throw your clothes in the wash."

"Don't worry," he said, hands on my shoulders, standing there in his boxers. "He's not gonna find out."

I gathered up his clothes and headed for the laundry room, trailing dirt behind me. He must have gone to the farm after dropping Angela off at his place. Bits of hay, dirt, manure?

The shower was running when I came back into the apartment. I picked up the phone book to find the number of a women's shelter and put it back down. I realized it wouldn't be listed in the phone book, but I knew there was one not far away. I sometimes dropped off clothing and other things.

A few minutes later, Chris stepped out of the shower, transformed, towel wrapped around his waist, hair dripping. Any other time, I would have pulled the towel from his waist and started making love to him. For a second, I thought about it.

"How long is she going to stay with you?" I asked.

"I don't know. She says he gets like this every now and again. He just needs time to cool off and then he's ok again."

"She'll go back? There's a women's shelter not far from here. You could take her there," I said.

"She won't go," he said.

"She called you a 'fuckin' knight in shining armour,'" I said. "You've rescued her before?"

"Yeah."

"Big Steve – drug dealer? Not just a rider, part of a riding club, maybe?" I asked. He couldn't very well say "none of your business" with a towel wrapped around his waist, could he?

"He was, at one time, part of a riding club, but got out a year ago or so."

"How do you know him?" I asked.

"You know," he said, shrugging his shoulders.

"No, I don't."

"I dealt a little pot back in the day. I needed to make some money."

"And now?"

"Just from time to time, when I'm short of cash".

My heart started racing. I imagined Big Steve showing up at my door looking for Chris, looking for Angie. He didn't know where I lived. Yet.

"You know, Big Steve actually tried to set up an art show for me a year or so ago. I showed him some of my art work and he was crazy about it. Said he could move it, no problem. His buddies would go nuts over it."

"What happened?"

"Two weeks before the show, I had about 70 pieces completed – sculptures, big and small, paintings of all sizes, gone."

"What?? Who do you think was behind that?" I asked.

"I don't know," he said. "I've always wondered if Big Steve had a hand in it. Decided to up and distribute my work and forgot to tell me about it. I don't know."

"And now you're rescuing his woman?"

"Don't worry. She's got a shift tonight. I said she could get cleaned up and rest at my place and then I'll drive her to work."

"You don't think Big Steve's gonna be waiting for you at the club?"

"I won't take her all the way to work. Just to the bus. Then I'll be back, ok?"

I went down to the laundry to put his clothes in the dryer and waited there until they were done.

***

The air was thick. I leaned in to the fan, lifted my shirt and felt the air against my clammy skin. A slight relief. I pulled my hair back and tied it into a knot, a look I saved for home. All the windows were open. I could see Fran across the way in her apartment; her kitchen was exactly opposite mine. Her laptop was open. She was wearing a big tented dress. It looked like one of those dresses I brought back from Hawaii every time I went. Flowy and cool. I waved.

I heard the first crack of thunder. The sky darkened. There was a knock at my door. I opened it.

"How did you get in?" I asked Chris.

"One of the old ladies in the building let me in. I talk to her on the street from time to time. Sally, I think her name is. Wanna go for a walk?"

"There's a storm brewing," I said.

"Exactly! Let's go."

"Ok." I pulled on my shoes, went to grab a jacket –

"You don't need that," he said.

"Yeah, you're right."

I loosened my hair. "I kinda like that look," he said. I laughed. "Different, sort of librarian-like, the knot. You got black-rimmed glasses hidden away somewhere?"

"Ha – you'll see," I said.

We walked out the door, as the next clap of thunder sounded. "Man, that sounds close," I said, as the first bolt of lightning struck. The first fat drops of rain fell.

"Let's head to the cemetery," he said.

"Really?" I said. "Won't that be rather creepy?"

"No, it'll be cool. It's the middle of the day," he said.

The sky was getting darker and darker. I had always hated cemeteries, but Mount Pleasant was really quite beautiful. On a bright sunny day, rollerbladers glided and cyclists cruised along the pathways and sometimes between the tombstones. And with Chris, I'd be fine, even in a thunderstorm. We took what had become our usual route, down Avenue Road to Davisville, then across the overpass. Chris now always stopped to pat the iron horse sculptures. He had named them Bob and Max.

"How ya doin', buddy?" he said, as he patted one, then the other. The overpass went over a set of subway tracks. The train rumbled underneath us. We made it to the other side before the rain started pelting down. It felt warm and sensuous. Chris grabbed my hand as we squeezed, one at a time, between the concrete pillar and the fence. The sky was now eerily dark. The clouds were angry. Lightning lit up the sky. I couldn't remember which trees to avoid in an electrical storm and which provided shelter and safety. Maybe none provided shelter. I dismissed the thought.

"Let's wait it out here," Chris said, heading toward the Eaton Mausoleum. "Hi, Tim," he said, raising his hand.

Concrete lions guarded the structure. We ran up the steps and sat huddled together, leaning against one of the concrete columns. Our legs touched. I could feel the heat of his body rising up through his pants to mine. He grabbed me and kissed me hard, then soft. The rain was bouncing off the sidewalks below us like ping pong balls. I felt protected there under the Eaton columns.

When the rain cleared and the sun came out, steam rose up from the grass and concrete. Within minutes, the walkways were dry, the air only slightly cooler. The tension dissipated.

"Thank-you, Mr. Eaton," Chris said as we left the mausoleum. "What are you doin' later?" he asked.

"I should do a bit of work. I have a class tomorrow I've got to prepare for," I said.

"Students coming tomorrow?"

"Yup – I've got sisters coming for language classes. Should be fun," I said.

"Why don't you come over when you're done?"

I hesitated. I had never been to his place. He just lived up the road. He had never invited me over, and I had never asked to see his place.

"Ok," I said.

"Just walk to the side of the house – you know which one it is – the one with the green outdoor carpet on the front steps - and knock on the side door. When do you think you'll come?"

"It's 4 now, how about around 6?"

"See ya then," he said.

Just before 6, I walked the two blocks to his house. As I came up the walk, I saw an elderly gentleman sitting on the front steps. "Hi," I said. He didn't say anything. He was wearing thick, thick glasses. Perhaps he didn't actually see me. I walked to the side of the house and saw that the screen door was open. I knocked lightly.

"Just a sec", I heard Chris say, then he appeared at the bottom of the stairs. "C'mon in," he said.

I headed down the stairs and was caught off guard by the smell of cat litter and wet dog. I gagged, but continued on down, holding my breath. The bathroom was at the bottom of the stairs. As I turned to go into the kitchen, I saw a litter box to the left in the bathroom and a birdcage on a small table. Bright blue budgies started chirping. A dog bowl sat on the floor near the fridge and next to it, a double bowl for the cat, containing remnants of food. The cat was up on the kitchen counter. My feline phobia kicked into high gear. The dog came toward me. My hands were in my pockets. I'm sure he sensed my nervousness. I had gone on many walks with Chris and Fred, but he was always leashed and under control. Fred was a strong, powerful dog and Chris had him well trained. Part Pitbull, part Pee Wee Hermann dog, he came up to me, wagging his tail. I patted him tentatively. When the cat nuzzled up against my legs, my entire body cringed. I stood there, paralyzed, but smiled and said, "So, this is where you live."

"Wanna drink?" he asked. "I've got beer, lemonade, water."

"Lemonade," I said. He opened the fridge. It was sparse. Beer, lemonade, a tomato, two eggs, a loaf of bread, a bottle of probiotics and a bottle of kelp.

"I eat out most of the time," he said.

"I gathered." He handed me a tall glass of lemonade. As I drank, I took in the rest of the apartment.

On the kitchen windowsill, I saw a wooden sculpture

of a woman. She stood about 12 inches tall. She was exquisite and exotic. A skirt draped around her waist, falling just above her knees. Bare breasts, a basket on her head, her right arm gracefully holding it. Her long hair fell to one side. The wood was dark. Mahogany, perhaps. A bottle of peanut oil stood beside her.

"Is this one of yours?" I asked.

"Yup."

"She's beautiful," I said.

"Yeah," he said, picking her up and running his hands over her. The way he touched her was so sensuous, tender and arousing.

Next to her sat a white polar bear. Sculpted to perfection out of marble. It was small and intricate. Every hair on its body sculpted in. The eyes, alive. Its body in mid-stride. I looked at Chris in awe. He stood there, hands on hips, smiling, watching me taking it all in.

"And this one?" I said, looking at an owl emerging out of a rock.

"Just coming alive," he said.

"How?" I said. "How did you learn to do this?"

"Self-taught, mostly," he said. "My grandfather was a carver. I used to watch him when I was a kid. He used to say to me, 'whatever needs to come out of the stone will show itself to you.' He died when I was quite young. I never really knew what he meant, until it happened to me. Now I'll get a piece of wood or stone and let it sit until I see something emerging from it. Then I get to work."

"Fascinating," I said. "Have you ever worked with jade?"

"No," he said.

I reached into my pocket and pulled out a piece of

green rock, a one-inch straight edge, half an inch across the top and curved toward the bottom, subtle white shadows running through it. "I thought you might find it interesting to work with," I said, handing it to him.

He turned it round and round in his hand, then rubbed one side of it with his thumb. "Hmm, it's got a nice feel to it. Smooth, hard, interesting colours. Don't know if I have the tools to work with it, but I'll give it a go." He slipped it into his front jeans pocket. "When we break up, I'll return it to you," he said, with a grin.

My stomach knotted. I leaned against the kitchen counter, turned away from him, and took a deep breath. At the edge of the counter sat a package of baggies and a small kitchen scale. My heart skipped a beat. What was he up to?

After a second or two, I turned back to see Chris holding the most intricate piece of all. A wooden carving of a wizened old man, skeletal, hunched over, wearing a loincloth, a staff in his hand and a smile on his face.

"May I?" I asked Chris.

"Go ahead," he said.

I took the carving and traced my index finger all around it, over the lines on his face, his thin arms, the staff. He looked like someone from Biblical times, a prophet.

"He's my starving old man," Chris said.

"I think he's wise and has a lot to offer," I said.

"Maybe. He's happy anyway," he said, chuckling.

I set the old man down gently, but couldn't take my eyes off of him for another few seconds. It was as if he held a closely-guarded secret, as though he knew something and wasn't going to let anybody in on it. I turned to see

Chris walk over to another door and pull it shut.

"Wanna get somethin' to eat?" he said.

"Yeah, sure," I said. "Got any place in mind?"

"How about Shoeless Joe's just up the road. They've got a good French Dip there." "Sure," I said, although I didn't really like roast beef.

"I've just got to feed the hound and we can go."

As soon as Chris started fiddling with the dog food, Fred came over to him, panting, eagerly waiting. Chris set the food down and said "wait" in a sharp tone. Fred stood back, looking at his master. "Go", he said, and Fred launched in. The cat meandered around looking for her bowl. He set it out for her as well. I stood back and watched this menagerie. The budgies were getting all excited now as well. Once the cat was fed, he walked over to the bird cage and refilled the water basins and topped up their food.

"We'll just take Fred for a quick walk around the block for a pee and we can go."

"Ok," I said.

"Maybe I'll just let him out in the back yard – 5 minutes or so."

"Ok," I said, amused.

"Christopher?" I heard someone call. I think it was the old man I had seen on the front steps.

"Yup, Uncle Frank?"

"There's a call for you," he said in a soft voice. He was standing at the top of the stairs, short-sleeved white shirt tucked neatly into his grey flannel trousers. He was not a tall man; there was a gentleness about him, the way he moved, slow measured steps. Maybe because of his thick glasses, maybe it was just his nature.

"Thanks," Chris said, picking up the phone at the bottom of the stairs. "I've got it," he shouted. Perhaps Uncle Frank was listening on the other end of the line upstairs.

"Yeah, go ahead," Chris said. He looked down at the floor, listening intently. "What time? Yeah, ok." He hung up the phone.

"Ok," he said, looking at me and grabbing my hand. "Let's go. C'mon Fred." The three of us trundled up the stairs, Fred trying to squeeze past us to the top. At the top of the stairs, Chris waited, hand on the doorknob. Fred looking at him eagerly. As soon as the door opened, Fred trotted out the door and found his favourite tree.

"What was that about?" slipped out of my mouth before I could stop myself.

"Business," he said. "Got an errand to run later."

I was dying to say "What kind of errand?", but thought better of it. Once Fred was safely back in the apartment, we walked up to Shoeless Joe's. It was Friday night and the bar was almost full. We found a small table in the centre of the room and sat down.

"Haven't seen you in a while," the waitress said to Chris, placing a hand on his shoulder.

"Been busy," he replied, grinning.

"We've got that French Dip on tonight, the one you love," she said. "Can I get you a beer while your friend here decides?"

"Yeah, sure," he said.

"For you?" she said, looking my way.

"Coor's Light," I said.

"Didn't figure you for a beer drinker," Chris said, looking at me.

"I'm really not – Coor's Light – hardly a real beer," I said, laughing. "I've never been here before. Walked by it a thousand times, but never been in."

"I'm here quite a bit," he said. "Don't really cook at home."

"The waitress seems to know you," I said.

"Yeah," he said, grinning sheepishly. "She always asks me to stay and have a drink while she closes."

"And, do you?" I asked.

"Once," I said, "but I didn't like where it was going, so I left."

"What do you mean?" I asked.

"I think she wanted me to go home with her. I wasn't feeling it," he said.

I looked toward the door when it opened.

A tall, heavier set woman walked into the bar, carrying a motorcycle helmet under her arm. She looked around the room. Her eyes came to rest on Chris. She walked over.

"I thought you might be here," she said, pulling up a chair next to Chris. She plopped her helmet down on the seat beside her. "Hi, I'm Angela," she said, looking at me.

"Hi," I said, shaking her hand. "I'm Sara."

"You the one I talked to on the phone the other day?"

"Yup."

"Hm. You're different."

"Different than what?" I said.

"Wanna beer?" Chris asked her. "Yeah, sure," she said.

"What's Steve up to tonight?" Chris asked.

"He'll be joining us shortly. That's what he said anyway."

"Here?" Chris said.

"I told him I was gonna stop in here," she said

shrugging out of her leather jacket. She was a lot bigger than I had imagined and broad-shouldered, dyed blond hair, dark roots showing, big teeth, not terribly well looked after. Her blue-grey eyes lit up when she smiled. It wasn't hard to imagine her with a black eye or somewhat beat up, but I couldn't quite picture any man having the gall to mess with her. She seemed like one tough broad.

"Jess," Chris called to the waitress.

"Yeah, sweetie," she said, placing one hand on his shoulder, the other holding a tray.

"A beer for Angie here," he said.

"Tap?" Angie nodded. "Comin' right up. You good?" she said, looking at Chris. "Your food order should be right up as well."

"Great," he said. She didn't pay any attention to me. My Coor's Light had gone rather warm.

***

He sat on the floor, on one side of the room, me on the other. He looked at me, really looked at me. I had to turn away. Something had shifted.

He moved toward me until he was kneeling in front of me, on the floor. He put his hands on my face and kissed me. A long, lingering kiss that coursed through my body like lightning, striking here and there. When he pulled away, I just stared at him. He grinned. And kissed me again. This time, I held his face in my hands and then stroked his hair, soft and silky. I wondered what kind of shampoo he used. I had never been with a man whose hair was longer than mine; felt a bit girly, it was strange and nice, all at the same time. I put my hands under his shirt and felt the strength of his body. His chest, his arms. Inhaled him. Slowly and deliberately, he unbuttoned my shirt, my jeans and explored every inch of me until I was ready to explode. With one hand, he took off his jeans, while I wrestled off his shirt. His body fit perfectly to mine, merging, melding. We lay there, like that, together, in a daze, for a long while. He rolled on to his side and stroked my face, my hair.

"Have you ever been in love?" he asked.

I didn't know what to say, because I was reeling. Had I been? I don't know. Lust or love? What was I in now?

"Really, truly in love? No," I said and then immediately regretted it. What if he felt I was incapable of falling in love? What if I was incapable of falling in love? I knew I was capable of loving. What was the difference? Shut-up I said to myself. Stop thinking.

"You?" I said.

"Yeah," he said. "My first love. I was crazy about her. She was my best friend, my lover..."

"That sounds like a Rod Stewart song," I said, laughing.

"What?"

"Never mind," I said. "You're lucky to have felt that. I don't know many people who have. What happened?"

"I don't know," he said. "We grew up, I guess, and drifted apart. You never get that back. I mean, I think you're capable of falling in love again, but it would be different."

"Of course," I said, "it has to be different, maybe better and deeper."

"What about you? You've really never been in love? I find that hard to believe." He looked at me closely, stroking my hair.

"Yeah? Why?" I asked.

"You're smart and funny, pretty too."

"Falling in love kinda works both ways, doesn't it? A two-way street? When I fall into something and the other doesn't, am I still falling in love? Maybe it's just infatuation and unrequited. The very worst kind of love, as Kate Winslet's character says in *The Holiday*.

"You really think things to death, don't you?" he said. "Why don't you just let yourself feel? Just follow your heart. Don't hang on so tight."

"Is that what you do?" I asked.

"I try," he paused for a second. "I try to live like that."

"What's the difference between that and living impulsively? Living for the moment, without any consequence?"

"Well, that's the beauty of it. You don't think about the consequence. Live in the moment. See where it takes you."

"And then?" I asked.

"You think too much," he said and kissed me hard and then soft, until I could feel myself melting into him again and falling. Consequences be damned, I thought and gave in to an evening of lovemaking and sensation and laughter.

I woke up at 3:00 am and saw that he was gone. No note, no trace of him, save the rumpled sheets on his side of the bed and the dent in the pillow. I rolled over and caught a whiff of Mennen Speedstick and smiled. The next time I looked at the clock it was 7:00 am; the phone was ringing.

"You up?" he asked, sounding bright.

"Barely," I said. "Where are you?"

"At my place. I just got back from the farm. It's a beautiful morning. Why don't you come out with me to the farm and we can go for a morning ride?"

"Bike or horse?"

"Both. We'll hop on the bike, ride to the farm and then jump on a couple of horses. It's a gorgeous morning, and I've got just the mare for you. Real gentle. C'mon – it'll be great!"

"Ok," I said, rolling out of bed.

"Great," he said. "I'll be over in 10 minutes."

After a quick rinse in the shower, I pulled my hair into a ponytail, slipped into a pair of capris, T-shirt, jean jacket, running shoes and I was off. I bounded out the door and down the stairs, and there he was, motorcycle running, a welcoming grin on his face.

"Look at you," he said, "I've never seen you get ready so quickly!"

"Live in the moment, right?" I said, laughing.

I felt like a kid. He strapped on the helmet for me, his face close to mine, his fingers just grazing my cheek and chin. I climbed on behind him and we were off, weaving in and out of traffic until we were up on Highway 7, green rolling hills on either side of us. There was still a bit of a chill in the air and it smelled so fresh and clean. I leaned in just a bit closer and wrapped my arms around him even tighter.

He slowed the bike and turned left into a long driveway. There was fencing on either side. A large ranch house came into view. As we drove past it, Chris waved to someone inside. He waved back. The driveway continued on to a couple of barns at the back of the property, two paddocks and a covered riding ring. Chris pulled up alongside one of the barns and cut the engine.

"Here we are," he said.

"Is this where you work?"

"Yup," he said. "See that one over there?"

He pointed to a beautiful roan coloured horse. "Isn't she gorgeous? She's a dream to work with. I had her out this morning. She seems to anticipate what I want her to do and does it, just with a nudge here and there. It's amazing. It's a language all its own."

"I've always been afraid of horses," I volunteered quietly.

"Why?"

"They're huge, for one. And, I've fallen off before."

"Oh, so you're not as unadventurous as you first seem," he said. "I thought there was more to you than met the eye. C'mon," he said, grabbing my hand.

What did that mean, I wondered, and the insecurities started coursing through my body. And horses could sense that, I'd been told.

"Now that one over there," he said, pointing to a smaller white horse. "She's really gentle. She'll just wait for you to tell her what to do."

"We'll likely be sitting here all day, then. I don't know what to do on a horse," I said. I could feel the panic setting in, rising up through my body, hands sweating. I wiped them on my pants.

"Ok, how about this? I'll get you up on the horse and walk you around the ring. Then, when you feel comfortable, we'll venture out into the field and go for a little ride."

"Ok, I'll give it a go," I said.

I watched as he approached the mare, slipped a halter

over her head in one fell swoop, held the lead in one hand and walked her toward me. I could hear him speaking softly to her as they walked. She had absolute confidence in him. She'd follow him anywhere.

"Just let her smell you for a minute," he said.

The mare touched my hand with her nose. My instinct was to pull away, but I resisted. Her nose felt soft and velvety against my skin. I could feel myself starting to smile. Chris grinned.

"Nice, isn't it?"

"Yeah," I said.

"Hold her for a minute, while I get the saddle," he said.

"Is that a good idea?" I said. "We're only just getting to know each other."

"You'll be fine. I'll just be a minute," he said.

"Ok," I said. I stood there holding the lead, looking at the horse, eyes on the barn, waiting for Chris to return. The horse started to walk. I didn't know what else to do, so I walked along with her. She was heading toward the barn. I thought about holding back the lead, like a dog leash, but she was so big.

Just then Chris came walking out of the barn, saddle slung over his shoulder, a big grin on his face, head down, waving his arm, as if to someone behind him. He looked up to see us coming toward him.

"What are you doing? Where are you going?" Grin disappeared.

"Uh, she started walking and I didn't know what else to do, so I went along with her," I said.

"You need to show her who's boss," he said.

"It's clearly not me!" I said, "And I know enough to know that horses can smell fear and anxiety a mile away."

"Hey girl," he said, speaking to the horse, rubbing the side of her face and then down her flank. "Let's get you saddled up."

"Here," he said, handing the lead to me. He hoisted the saddle up on to her back in one motion, firmly, but gently. He was prattling on to her the whole time.

"There," he said, once everything was in place. "Let me help you up," he said, holding out his hand.

I placed my left foot in the stirrup and swung my right leg over her back. Man, she was big and tall.

"Ready?" Chris said.

"Ready as I'll ever be," I said, taking a deep breath.

"Just relax," he said, and started walking the horse and me around the ring. I felt like a kid.

From my perch, I watched him interact with the horse and saw just how comfortable he was. I felt slightly envious. I reached down with my right hand and just rubbed her neck.

"There ya go," he said. "You'll be fine."

The cool crisp morning was turning into a warm summer's day. After about 20 minutes, I had had enough.

"Why don't you ride her for a bit?" I suggested to Chris.

"Had enough?" he said.

"Yeah, for now," I said.

He helped me down and mounted her with ease. He took the reins in his hands and with a tug here and a nudge with his thighs there, they were off. Horse and rider as one; his long ponytail flying behind him. He looked a bit like the Lone Ranger, without the mask.

They left the riding ring and galloped out into the fields. I stood there at the side of the ring and watched until they disappeared from sight. I looked around the property, wandered back to the barn. A young woman was mucking out stalls, her sandy blonde hair done up in a messy braid.

She looked up from under her Blue Jays baseball cap. "Hey," she said.

"Hi."

"You here with Chris?" she said.

"Yeah," I said. "He wanted me to try to ride the roan, but I think she's a bit big for me."

"He said he was going to bring someone around. That's my horse," she said.

"I'm not very comfortable around horses," I said. "And he's just a natural."

"He sure is."

"How long has he worked here?" I asked.

"It's been a while," she said. "He works with our other horses, mostly with the race horses. I'm just here in the summer, so I don't really know a lot of the farmhands. He's cool."

"Where'd he go?" she asked.

"Just wanted to go for a ride with her."

"Did he take the saddle off?" she asked.

"No. Why?"

"Sometimes he just likes to jump on and go. The horses are so comfortable with him, they love it. He disappears for hours sometimes," she said.

"Oh," I said. "Well, let's see what happens today."

"I'm about done here," she said, giving the stall a final once-over, then wiping her hands on her jodhpurs.

"Were you out riding earlier?" I asked.

"Yeah, I usually take one of the horses out first thing

in the morning, then come back, brush it down and muck out the stalls. I've gotta go. I'm sure he won't be gone too long," she said with a laugh.

I walked from one end of the barn to the other, then back out to the paddocks. I climbed up onto the fence and sat there a while, looking out over the fields. It was warm now. I closed my eyes and let the sun warm my face. And then I saw him in the distance, riding towards me. Galloping hard. Wow, it must feel nice – it felt nice just watching him. He rode right up next to me, so we were at the same height. He leaned in toward me and kissed me. Just like that.

"What was that for?" I asked, laughing.

"Just felt like it," he said. "I'll take her into the barn, give her a rub-down and we can get going." He gave the horse a little nudge with his heels and off they went.

"Ok."

I walked over and met them in the stall.

"By the way," he said, peering up from behind the horse, "there's a party at Steve and Angela's on Friday. Wanna go?"

"Any special occasion?"

"No, just a get-together."

"Yeah, ok," I said.

As Friday drew closer, I began to feel a little anxious. I had yet met to meet Steve; he didn't show that night in the bar. Everything I had heard made me nervous. I had an image of a big burly man, at least 6 feet tall, wearing a pair of worn jeans, a plaid shirt tucked into his jeans, and a beer gut that hung over his pants, suspenders, a scruffy beard, maybe even sporting a bandana. A Harley, of course, and someone who was one moment real sweet with his wife and the next, ready to take a swing at her. But I had been wrong before.

"What can you tell me about Steve?" I asked Chris.

"He's a real nice guy," he said, "but you wouldn't want to get on his bad side."

"What does he do?" I asked.

"He's self-employed," he said. "A little construction, renovations, that sort of thing."

"And the pot, right?" I suddenly remembered.

"What's with all the questions?"

"I just wanna know what I'm walking into," I said.

"You'll just have to wait and see."

"Where does he live?"

"Jesus – what is it with you?"

I cringed.

"I don't grill you about your friends."

"That's true, but then, you've never expressed any interest in meeting them either," I said quietly.

"When have I said that? What are you talking about?"

"Well, just any time I mention them, like Annie, one of my closest friends, or..." My voice trailed off.

"I think I'll get going," he said. "I'll call you later."

"What time on Friday?"

"So you are coming then?"

"Yeah, I'll come," I said, ignoring the red flags and bells going off inside me.

"I'll come by around 7," he said, and walked out the door.

***

It was one of those warm, sultry nights where everything is hot and sticky; a night where the slightest vibration or hum of an engine is arousing and a touch electrifying.

It took us about an hour to drive north of the city in weekend traffic. We were somewhere near Barrie. I thought it would cost at least $60 or $80 to take a cab home, if I needed to leave. I made sure I had enough cash with me. We turned into a gravel driveway, maple trees on either side. As we approached the house, I could see the Harleys lined up to the right. We pulled up to the left and parked the orange Plymouth Duster there.

I wiped my hands on my jeans. I could hardly breathe, and we hadn't even entered the party.

"C'mon, let's go," Chris said, grabbing my hand.

"Ok," I said, a smile barely escaping my lips. There was a group of people standing on the porch, beer in one hand, cigarette or joint in the other.

"I've gotta get you a drink," Chris said. "Just loosen up, will ya?"

Just then Angela came bounding out of the house, her breasts bouncing and straining her pale yellow halter top.

"I was hoping you'd get here soon," she said, grabbing Chris and giving him a big kiss. "Sara, was it?" she said looking at me.

I nodded. "Hi", I said.

"C'mon in, grab a drink. Steve's gonna be so happy to see you," she said, looking at Chris.

"Oh yeah? Why is that?"

"I'll let him tell you," she said. "He's just over there."

I looked to where she motioned. There he was, Big Steve, holding court, the biker boys all around him. He wasn't as tall as I had imagined, but he was built like a bulldog, muscled, fitter than I thought he would be. Long, curly dark hair framed his face. Just then his eyes met mine. It was just a second, but the look was hard and cold, and suddenly he smiled. I turned away.

"Sara, why don't you come with me? Meet some of the other guys and their girls," Angela said.

"Yeah, ok."

"Do you mind if I just use the bathroom?" I asked.

"Sure, sweetie, it's just over there, second door on your left."

I walked down the hall and glanced into the first room. It was a bedroom, messy, unmade bed, clothes flung all over the place. I looked to my right. The linen closet was slightly ajar. Mismatched towels, sheets and pillowcases all askew, blankets. Out of the corner of my eye, I saw a wooden sculpture, a horse. I gently moved the sheet aside and drew it out, glancing down the hall to make sure no one was watching me. It was beautiful. Dark wood, it might have been cherry, the horse in mid-gallop, straining, the mane and tail etched in detail, not unlike the polar bear in Chris's kitchen. I turned the sculpture over and there it was, CS, roughly carved, his initials. As I put it back, I saw there were others. I wondered how deep the closet was.

"You lost there?" I heard a big voice behind me. I turned to see Steve coming toward me. "If you're looking for the bathroom, it's the next door on your left."

"Thanks," I said brightly. "I was just looking for a hand towel."

"There should be one in the bathroom," he said. "And who are you?"

"Sara," I said, extending my hand to shake his. His handshake was weak, not what I expected. He was about my height, 5'7", square build, a moustache that crept into his mouth.

"You here with Chris?" he asked. I nodded.

"Good guy," he said.

"He says the same thing about you," I said, allowing myself to smile.

His eyes softened slightly. "See ya back out there," he said, as I walked into the bathroom.

I wondered how many of Chris's sculptures he had hidden away in his house and why. I closed the bathroom door and locked it. I found myself going through the vanity and then the cupboards below the sink, but I didn't find any more. There was a knock on the door.

"Sara?" It was Chris. "You in there?"

"Yeah, be out in a minute."

I flushed the toilet, washed my hands, wiped them on my jeans, unlocked the door and opened it. "I wondered where you went," he said.

"Here I am," I said and kissed him lightly. He grinned and grabbed my hand, then my left butt cheek and drew me to him. I could feel him up against me and me melting into him. I loved that about him. How we fit so well together.

"Let's go back in," he whispered.

"Into the bathroom?"

"Yeah. Just quickly."

He moved me gently backwards, kissing me all the way, until we were on the other side of the door, closed it with his foot and locked it with his hand behind his back. He sat down on the toilet seat and pulled me on top of him, rocking my hips just the way he liked it. The heat of the night, the humidity in the air, the sweat. All either of us needed was the slightest touch of the other to come. We sat there, like that, for a few minutes, holding each other.

"I guess we should get back out there," he said, gently moving me off of him.

"Or we could just leave," I said.

"We should at least stay for a drink," he said.

"Yeah, ok," I said. We cleaned ourselves up and went back to the deck.

"So, did you find what you were looking for?" Steve said, looking at me.

"Yeah," I said, looking up at Chris and smiling. "I sure did."

"You better watch that one," Steve said quietly to Chris. "I think she's trouble."

"Hmmm," Chris uttered.

Just then Angela stood up onto a chair and called us to attention.

"I've got an announcement to make," she said, raising her glass.

The room went quiet. "Everybody got a drink?"

All around the room, I could hear the distinct sound of beer cans opening, and bottle caps twisting.

"Me and Steve are gonna have a baby!!!" she said, squealing. All through the room, there were shouts of excitement and congratulations. "Drink up everyone," she said. The guys high-fived Steve. He was grinning from ear to ear. The girls crowded around Angela. I hung back a bit. I was thinking of her beat up outside the strip club and the man who had done it to her.

We were just making our way down the stairs, when

Steve called out to Chris.

"Thanks, buddy."

"Yup," Chris said. "Hey, and congratulations!"

"Thanks, man," he said, shaking Chris's hand and pulling him into a half man-hug.

"What's that about?" I asked.

"Just some business stuff," he said.

"And none of mine, I guess," I said. He just grinned and nodded. "Hey look," I said, pointing to a room off to the side. "A pool table. "Come on, let's play."

"Yeah, ok," he said.

I racked up the balls, placed the 8 ball in the centre, lined the rack up on the centre point, and removed it. "Do you want to break, or shall I?"

"Go ahead," he said, laughing.

I grabbed the pool stick with authority, placed it on the edge of the table between my thumb and forefinger, slid it back and forth and kapow, hit the cue ball with just the right amount of force to send the balls in every direction. The stick felt solid in my hands; I had managed to hit the sweet spot. Chris was a bit gobsmacked. "Oh ho", he said, "So, that's how we're gonna play it. Well, let's see." He managed to get the stick up onto the edge of the table, positioned himself, wiggled his bum back and forth like a baseball player, and hit the cue ball with just enough strength to move it along and kiss one of the striped balls.

"Ha," I thought to myself and shoved him out of the way. With just a gentle nudge, I coaxed the ball into the pocket. "Stripes," I yelled out. Cautiously, I proceeded to line up my next target. And got it into the side pocket. Next... I moved to the side of the table and tried a move my Dad had taught me. I placed the stick behind my back, positioned it on the edge of the table with my right arm behind my back, slipped the stick between the thumb and forefinger of my left hand, gently slid it back and forth and hit the cue ball. It hit the green striped ball with just the right amount of weight and strength and in it went, into the corner pocket. A little crowd started to gather around the table.

'What have we got here?" I heard someone say.

"A little pool shark?"

"Who woulda thought?" A small group had gathered.

I ignored them all and kept playing. Until there was one striped ball left. Chris was standing there, leaning on his pool stick, smiling. I looked at him for a sec, wearing his striped T-shirt, half-tucked into his jeans, scruffy running shoes, hair pulled back into a long ponytail, bright hazel eyes just lookin' at me, grinning. I smiled back and popped the last striped ball into the side pocket. "8 ball? Into that corner," I said, pointing to the top left corner pocket. I felt the stick firmly in my left hand, slid it back and forth twice, and hit the cue ball. With a satisfying plop, the 8 ball landed where I had predicted it would.

"That's me done," Chris said. "Anyone else wanna give it a try?"

"I'll give it a go," said Steve, swaggering up to the table, swinging a beer in one hand, grabbing a pool stick with his other. His eyes were hard and glassy.

I grimaced and swallowed hard. I looked at Chris.

"You'll be fine," he said. I wasn't so sure.

"Rack 'em up," Steve bellowed. "And somebody get the lady a shot!"

"No thanks," I said.

"Ya play with me, ya drink."

"I guess that's me out, then," I said, feeling the dread and fear well up inside me. My hands were beginning to sweat and I knew I wouldn't be able to play worth beans in that state.

"Just have one," Chris whispered to me, "and that will satisfy him".

"Where's the bottle?" Steve demanded. "Slim, give him the bottle!" someone yelled. Steve grabbed the bottle, poured a shot and slammed it on the side of the pool table. I raised the glass, looked him in the eye, put it up to my mouth and shot it past my mouth, into a plant behind me. I hate shots. He was too drunk and stoned to notice.

"Break the balls, little lady," he yelled. "Break da balls, did ya hear what I just said?" and he threw back his head and laughed.

I positioned the stick, once again, and held it firmly between the thumb and forefinger of my left hand. I tried to drown out the sound of the gathering crowd. "You break those balls!" I kept hearing. "You go, girl!" I kept my stomach tight, and took a deep breath to calm my nerves. Kept telling myself, he's drunk, he's not gonna hurt me, I can always leave. I can just lose and that will be that.

With the force in my belly, I cracked the rack of balls wide open, but none went in. Steve, with fierce determination in his eyes, grabbed his stick and hit the cue ball so hard that it cracked two solids and sent them into opposite pockets. "Ya see that?" he said, looking right at me with his glazed eyes. "Now that's how it's done!"

"Good job," I managed to say.

"Now, let's see," he said, leaning on his stick, hands curled around it, long curls falling into his eyes. He pulled one hand away from the stick to push the hair out of his eyes. "I think I'll go for that one," he said, pointing to the red solid ball in the centre of the table. He lined up his stick and just then, one of his buddies, nudged his arm from behind, causing the cue ball to dribble down the table and hit nothing.

"What the hell?" he yelled, looking around. First he looked at me, but I was on the other side of the table. "Which one o' you bastards did that?" He looked at Chris.

"Don't look at me, buddy," he said.

"You afraid I might beat your little lady?" he roared. "Or, think I can't?"

He started to take a swing at Chris.

"Take it easy, buddy," Chris said. "It's just a game. I didn't do nothin'. Must o' been one of your other friends."

"Just take another shot," I said from the other side of the table.

"Ya think I can't take you either? Just watch me," he said.

"You know what?" I said. "I think I need to go."

"Oh no, you don't. You stay right there until we've played this thing out. I told you she was trouble," he said to Chris.

I looked at Chris. I didn't know what to do. I was scared.

He came around to my side of the table, put his arm around me and moved me toward the door.

"Woose!" Steve yelled, thrashing his stick around. "And don't forget what we talked about, ya hear?"

"Hey, man, take it easy," Chris said, moving past him as he ushered me out of the pool room and back into the living room.

"You ok?" Chris asked.

"No, but I will be. Let's just get out of here. Oh wait, we should just say good-bye to Angela," I said, my voice shaking.

"Why don't I do that? You go on ahead and wait for me in the car."

"Ok," I said and slipped unnoticed past the crowd in the living room and on through the group gathered on the porch.

"Headin' out already?" Slim said. "Great game you played in there. Never mind Steve. He just gets a little excited. He's super stoked about knockin' up his woman. And he doesn't like it when any woman shows him up."

I smiled tentatively. "Catch ya next time," I said, and headed toward the car.

Chris stopped briefly to chat with the guys on the porch, waved and made his way to me.

"That was intense," I said, once Chris was in the car.

"Yeah," he said. "He's really ok, just gets a bit riled up, especially when he drinks and does drugs. You ok? Hey, I never knew you could play like that."

"We had a pool table growing up. Hey, thanks for taking care of me back there. Kinda cool. Knight in shining armour," I said, stroking his face.

Chris started the car and headed down the drive. It was still early for a summer's night. Just about 9:30 and dusk was setting in, the sky beautiful shades of pinks and oranges and purples, as though somebody had taken a paintbrush and swept across the sky with broad strokes.

"Geez, I can't imagine those two having a kid," I said. "What sort of life will it have, growing up in that environment?"

"Don't be so judgmental," he said. "They're actually

really nice people. Just be happy for them."

"It's not that I'm not happy for them. I just think of that night in my apartment when you were 'seeing' her somewhere, hurt and you wanted to help her. And Steve, I don't get a good feeling offa him at all. Not from the moment I saw him. I'd hate to get on the wrong side of that fist."

Chris didn't say anything.

"By the way, I came across some of your work at their house," I said.

"What do you mean?" he asked.

"Your sculptures."

"Steve doesn't have any of my sculptures."

"Well, I picked one of them up and it had CS carved into the bottom. I've seen those same initials on your other stuff."

"What was it of?

"A horse, dark wood, in mid-gallop."

He was quiet. "What are you thinking?" I said. He slowed the car right down and pulled over onto the side of the road and put his head on the wheel of the car. I put my hand on his back. He shrugged it away.

"I feel like I've been kicked in the gut," he said, turning his head to the right to look at me. "Were there others?"

"Yeah. I don't know how many, but it looked like there were more. And Steve saw me."

"Shit! Oh shit, shit shit!" he said, banging his hand on the wheel.

"I told him I was looking for a hand towel."

"Did he believe you?"

"I think so. Actually, I don't know, but I was on my way to the bathroom, so ...maybe.

What's the deal with him anyway?"

"Fuck ... you're so bloody nosy!"

My body tensed up.

"Look, I'm here with you. I've gotta be honest, the guy freaks me out just a bit and you're in some sort of business dealings with him, I'm guessing. I don't know why you're defending him. What's he got on you?"

"I don't want to get you involved. The less you know the better."

He pulled back onto the road and headed toward Highway 400. We drove back to the city in silence.

"You coming in?" I asked, as we pulled up in front of my building.

"No. I've still got to walk Fred," he said.

"Ok. Good night, then," I said, and leaned over to kiss him on the cheek.

He didn't say anything and pulled away the moment the car door closed. I watched the car pull up toward the red traffic light, proceed through the green, past his house and over the hill. What about Fred? I wondered.

I felt relieved to be back in my apartment. I plugged in the kettle. While I waited for it to whistle, I scooped out a teaspoon of Earl Grey tea leaves and placed them in the tea strainer. I didn't want to think. I just wanted to pretend that we hadn't been at the party, that I didn't know anything about Steve and Angela, that I hadn't seen the sculptures and that they weren't having a baby!

I suddenly felt so tired. I lay down on the bed, drew a pillow close to me and curled around it.

The continuous ringing of the apartment buzzer woke me. What the hell? I hoped it wasn't somebody ringing everybody's buzzer in the hope of being let into the building. Uggghhhh. I pressed the "talk" button.

"Hello?"

"Can you open the door?" Chris said.

I pressed the "door" button without saying anything. I heard it open and slam shut. I opened the door to my apartment and there he stood, holding a box.

"What is it?" I asked.

"I didn't want to believe you when you said you saw one or more pieces at Steve's house," he said, shaking his head.

"You went back?"

"Yeah – I drove around to the back of his house, saw that the party was still in full swing and looked in his garage. I didn't find anything there, but then I saw the garden shed. It was locked, but I managed to open it quite easily. In a box, under some shelving, I found these." He opened the box and there they were – an eagle in flight, each feather carved in detail, talons out, ready to pounce. The most beautiful owl carved out of rock, eyes intense. Horses sculpted out of that same dark wood I had seen in the closet.

"Why would he do this?"

Chris looked at me, then looked down, his hands in his pockets. "I owe him some money," he said. "Quite a lot, actually."

I didn't say anything.

"The thing he wanted to talk to me about tonight? That was about moving some product. He wants to move me up the ladder, promote me so to speak, so that I get a bigger cut, but it's also riskier."

"So how does that work exactly? You're obviously talking about something illegal." My heart was racing, palms sweaty. "So what now? What's going to happen when he finds out the box is missing?"

"I don't know. I just needed to find out what he did. Now I need to know where the rest of the stuff is. I had way more than this. Much bigger pieces too."

"Let me get this straight. He didn't say to you, give me your sculptures as collateral until you come up with the cash and in the meantime, you can work for me?"

"Not in so many words. I never thought he would just steal them," he said.

"That day when I discovered they were missing – you know, I went to the shop where I'd been working on them – I just wanted to finish up a couple of things before my show – I unlocked the shed and all I saw were a few tools, mostly empty shelves, one or two small pieces left here and there – all that work, I just felt sick. I felt so sick," he said.

"Do you have any photographs of the work?"

"No, I don't have any fuckin' photographs of the work."

"I'm sorry, I'm just trying to help," I said quietly.

"I know," he said, coming toward me, wanting to be held. "I don't know what to do. He must have the rest as well or at least know where it is."

"How much do you owe him?" I asked.

"About ten grand," he said.

"That's a lot of money," I said.

"Yeah – it's like he's holding my work hostage."

"And you," I said.

"Yeah, and me. It's weird though, because the guy who was letting me use his shop to work on this stuff introduced me to Steve. I mean, I was having some money problems at the time, meaning I didn't have any," he said, laughing nervously, "and I had some debt."

"So, Steve loaned you some money."

"Yeah. I was supposed to pay him back in 25% installments, starting a few months back, and when I couldn't, he asked me if I wanted in on some business deals with him. What could I say?"

"No would have been good," I said.

"Yeah, but... anyway, I was hoping to sell some of my shit. Had visions of being able to unload it at a good price and then, gone."

"Can I leave these with you?" he asked.

I hesitated. "Uhhhh..."

"Never mind. Forget I asked."

"It's just that ..."

"It's ok. I'll figure it out."

"Ummm, well, we could store them in my locker in the garage, next to my car. Or maybe at the farm where you work?"

"No, that wouldn't work. The garage is good."

"Do you think he's got your bigger pieces stashed somewhere as well?"

"I dunno. I don't really want to think about it. It makes me sick to think about it."

"What do you need to do for Steve and how much money will you make? Is he good for it? I mean, will he give you your cut of whatever it is?"

"He's kept his word so far. But it's just been a couple hundred bucks here and there. This is different."

"Oh. When do you have to start?"

"I'm not going to tell you, because I don't want you involved."

"For God's sake, I am involved! Can't you see? Let's go put this box in the garage."

"You know what? I'll just take it home in the morning. I'm gonna have a shower and go to bed."

"Ok," I said, feeling slightly relieved.

The next morning when I woke up, he was gone. So was the box of sculptures. I puttered around most of the day. I walked by his house and couldn't see the orange Duster parked anywhere. He'd be home at some point to walk Fred, though, I was sure of that.

I didn't hear anything from him that day or the next day or the day after that. The days turned into weeks. I toyed with the idea of going to the police. Then I thought of calling Angela to see if she had heard from him. I thought about going to the strip club where she worked, but couldn't quite see myself doing that. Didn't actually know the name of it. The thought of seeing Steve sent chills up and down my spine. The cold, hard look in his eyes had stayed with me. I had visions of Chris being holed up somewhere or killed. I wondered if I would ever see him again.

Six weeks after he left my apartment, I received a parcel in the mail. No return address. A large padded envelope, addressed to me in an almost illegible scrawl. I tore it open, tugging away at the bubble wrap. A beautiful set of wooden salad utensils emerged from the bubble wrap. A beaver, its paws gripping the branch handle, its pelt etched in detail, sat at the top of each utensil, its mouth open, eager to gnaw through the wood. I turned the utensils over and there, carved into the wood, were the initials CS.

***

"You might want to take some time to discuss this with your family," Dr. Schönberg said, as she completed the notes in my file, "before you make a decision."

"It's definite, then?" I asked.

"Yes, blood tests don't lie. You're about six weeks along. What about the father?"

"I don't know. I mean, I know who the father is, but I don't know if he'll be in the picture. And besides, he's out of town now, and I don't know how to reach him."

She stopped writing in my file and looked up at me, her bright blue eyes meeting mine. She rolled back her chair to face me.

"It might be even more important to speak with your family then," she said. She picked up her yellow HB pencil and twirled it between her fingers. "Raising a child on your own is no mean feat. Many people do it, but it's not easy."

I nodded. I could feel the tears coming and a lump forming in my throat.

"Talk to your family," she said again. "I'm going to schedule an ultrasound for you, and, if you decide not to go through with this, you can always cancel the appointment."

"Thank you," I said, swinging my legs over the side of the exam table.

"It'll be ok," she said, placing her hand on my shoulder.

I managed to smile. She grabbed my file and opened the door to leave. "I'll get my receptionist to arrange that ultrasound for you. Stop by her desk on your way out."

I nodded. When the door closed behind her, I removed the gown and took a moment to look at my body. No sign of anything. Flat stomach. I had worked so hard at that. I held my hands there for a moment. Couldn't possibly imagine what I would look like in 6-7-8 months' time. But I also couldn't imagine not going through with this.

I slowly got dressed. My jeans fit perfectly, not a bump in sight, shirt tucked in, no one would ever guess. I stopped at the receptionist's desk and picked up the slip of paper with the ultrasound appointment. Thursday, September 2nd at 2:00 pm. Two short weeks away.

"Once you've had the ultrasound," the receptionist said, "the doctor will refer you to a specialist".

"Why?" I asked.

She looked down at her desk and then back up at me. "Once you hit 35 and you're having your first baby, there are certain risks, and it's better to be in the care of a specialist."

"Oh," I said, folding the slip of paper over and over again.

Maybe I could just ignore everything. Maybe it was all a dream, and in the morning, I would see blood in my underwear, breathe a sigh of relief and say a silent prayer of thanks that all was back to normal.

But the blood didn't appear, the jeans got tighter, and no amount of biking, exercising, or running made any difference.

And still no word from Chris. I didn't want to contact his friends. I went to Shoeless Joe's a couple of times, thinking I might run into Angie and Steve – not that I wanted to, but I thought they might know something. Or even Jessica, the waitress. Maybe he had been in, but didn't want to see me.

"You here by yourself?" Jessica asked. "Where's your

fella?"

"Haven't seen him in a few weeks," I said. "Have you?"

"Uh, no," she said, "last time I seen him, he was with you. So, what'll ya have? Coor's Light?"

"Good memory. Yeah, sure," I said, "and water." I didn't really want to drink, but didn't want to say why, just in case someone Chris knew did come in.

"Here ya go," Jessica said, placing a coaster on the bar and the can of Coor's Light on top of it. "And one water. Want me to tell him you're lookin' for him if he shows up?"

"Yeah, sure," I said.

"What was your name again?" she said.

"Sara," I said.

"He's one of a kind, your fella," she said.

"What do you mean?"

"Well, he strikes me as someone who has integrity, is loyal to his friends and doesn't cheat," she said, a smile playing on her lips. "It used to be fun to flirt with him."

"Yeah," I said. My right hand was cold and wet from hanging on to the beer can. "I've gotta go," I said. "How much do I owe you?"

"But you haven't even touched your beer," she said. "

"Never mind, I've just gotta go. Will this cover it?" I put a $10 bill on the table.

"More than," she said. "You ok?"

"Yup," I said. I suddenly ached for him. Where had he gone? Who was he with?

When I got home, I hunted for the padded envelope which had contained the carvings. I found it under a pile of papers on my desk. I tried to make out the markings on the postage stamp, name of a city or town or even the date. It was smeared, likely from the rain or just the ink. I grabbed a magnifying glass. Still couldn't make it out. I tossed the envelope aside. He knew where to find me.

I picked up the telephone to call Annie. I hadn't talked to her since I'd started seeing Chris, but I was desperate to talk to someone. She picked up after a few rings.

"Annie!" I said. "How are you? It's me, Sara."

"Good. Yeah, everything's fine. Tell me, what's going on with you?" she said.

"Well, that's what I wanted to talk to you about, but not over the phone. Do you have time for lunch?"

"Yes, what time?"

"Whatever works for you," I said. "I'm very flexible today."

"Let me have a look here. How about 1:30, or how about I leave early and we meet at 3:00 for coffee down at Café Metropole? Then I don't have to worry about coming back to work," she said.

"Perfect," I said. "I'll see you there."

At 2:30, I left my apartment and headed toward the Davisville subway station. I glanced at the overpass, happy to see the metal horse sculptures. I half expected Chris and Fred to appear along the Beltline Trail, but it was empty. I arrived at the restaurant just before 3:00pm. Annie was already seated at a table for two.

"Hi, there," I said, giving her a big side squeeze. "It's so good to see you."

"C'mon, sit down," she said. "They offered me a table outside, but remember last time we were here? There was a bug in your salad."

"Yeah, and then we didn't have to pay for it." We laughed.

"So, tell me, what's new?" she said, her piercing blue

eyes staring into mine.

"Can we order first?" I said.

"No, tell me what's going on first."

I looked down at my legs, rubbed my hands on my faded jeans, looked up again.

"You're pregnant, aren't you?" she said.

"How did you know?"

"I could just feel it. This is fantastic! What a gift!" She looked like she was about to explode with joy.

I smiled, then started to laugh.

"And the father?" she said. "Does he know? Is he around?"

"Um, no. I don't know where he is at the moment."

"Perfect!" she said. "You're living my dream!"

"What? What do you mean?"

She leaned in to me. "It was always a fantasy of mine to seduce someone for an evening. You know, have a great meal, some wine, make wild passionate love, get pregnant, and never see him again. Wouldn't that be fantastic? You could raise your child the way you want, with no interference. No one questioning your judgement and no one telling you what to do. It's perfect!"

"Perfect in your dreams, maybe," I said.

"Have you told your parents?"

"NO!" I said. "They're so conservative when it comes to this type of thing. How will they look in the eyes of the church? A child out of wedlock and all that."

"Don't be silly. They will be thrilled."

"Let's order," I said, laughing. "I don't feel like salad today. You know what I love to eat here? Coffee and Apfelstrudel with vanilla custard. It's so decadent and delicious!"

"You should have it. I'll have the same," she said. "You need to eat now. Make sure you get enough calories. You're way too thin. How far along are you? 8 weeks or so?"

"About, yes," I said.

She smiled and then laughed until her whole body shook. "This is just wonderful," she said, clasping her hands in glee.

Our coffees came, along with a generous helping of Apfelstrudel and glorious vanilla custard on the side. I dug right in. Just as I remembered it. Crispy phyllo pastry, thinly sliced apples with cinnamon and a dollop of custard, all coming together in one fantastic taste and textural sensation.

"You know how I would break the news to your family? I would tell them Christmas Eve. How fitting would that be? Mary and the Baby Jesus. After all, Mary wasn't married."

I almost choked on my coffee. "You can't be serious," I said.

"Listen, a child is coming into the world. This is a gift!"

I smiled and mopped up the rest of the vanilla custard. Annie carried on about pre-natal vitamins and diet, but I wasn't really listening.

"Check please," Annie said, when our waitress passed our table.

"Let's just half it," I said.

"Oh no," she said. "It's not every day I get news like this!"

"Thank-you," I said.

As we left the café, she hugged me and said, "It's gonna be ok. You'll see. And you'll keep me posted, yes?"

"Of course," I said, hugging her again.

I joined the rest of the subway riders, moving en masse down the stairs to the platform and squeezed onto the next northbound train. I held on to one of the poles, closed my eyes and let my body jostle and rock along with the motion of the train. The train emerged from the underground into brilliant sunshine. I moved toward the exit and waited for the train to come to a complete stop. It was a gorgeous autumn day. With a sudden burst of energy, I ran up the stairs to street level and headed towards home. I avoided Yonge Street, took Davisville, then north up Avenue Road. The chestnut trees were brilliant in the afternoon sun.

My apartment block was the second of five non-descript yellow brick buildings. Bright red salvia still bloomed in the front garden and the pink and purple impatiens were hanging on, likely until the autumn winds came. The flower garden was the only thing that stood out amongst the five buildings. I waved to Sally, who was puttering around in the flower bed.

"Sara," she called out. I waved in acknowledgement.

"Sara," she called again.

I didn't really feel like chatting with her, but didn't want to be rude.

"Hi," I said, as I got closer to her.

"We missed you at the Garden Committee Meeting last night," she said.

"That was last night?" I said. "It completely slipped my mind."

"Not to worry. We covered everything and I'll send through the notes. By the way, I haven't seen your fella around lately. Everything ok there?"

"Do you know Chris?" I asked.

"Oh sure. We used to see him walking past with Fred all the time. My husband, Archie, loves that dog. They always have a little chat when they meet up on the street. And Archie's always got a treat for Fred. I've noticed him coming in and out of your building and figured it might be you he was comin' to see."

"Yup," I said.

"So, haven't seen him in a while."

"He's just out of town for a bit," I said.

"Didn't think he was much of a traveller," she said. "What does he do again?"

"A little of this and a little of that," I said.

"Oh, now, don't hold out on me. I remember now. He sculpts, right? He's shown me a piece or two. There was a polar bear he was workin' on. Just beautiful. So detailed. The eyes, each hair. It looked so alive. He's so talented. Does he still have it, do ya know?"

"I don't know," I said.

"Well, say 'hi' to him next time ya see him. Tell him I miss seeing him around."

"Will do," I said and made my way to my building.

Wouldn't Sally have loved to hear I was pregnant? Something to chat about with all the neighbours. I supposed I couldn't keep it secret for long, although I would have liked to.

I felt uneasy as I walked up the steps of my building. I stopped to check the mailbox. It was empty. I unlocked the apartment door and dropped the set of keys in the process. I opened the door. Something was amiss. I kicked off my shoes, and when I looked down, I saw a familiar pair of sneakers. Worn and dirty, the red stripe hardly visible anymore.

"Chris?" I said cautiously.

I walked through the kitchen and into the bedroom. There he was, on his back, legs splayed, chestnut coloured hair in a messy ponytail, fast asleep on the bed. My heart pounding, I lay down beside him. I didn't want to wake him, but what the hell was going on? I was so relieved to see him. He looked so peaceful lying there. I just stared at him. I rolled over on to my side.

The warm afternoon sun streamed into the bedroom. It wasn't long before I drifted off to sleep. When I awoke, he was awake, his arm across my body. I rolled over to face him.

"Hi," he said.

"Hi, yourself," I said. "I didn't expect to ever see you again."

"Hmmm, I'm like a dog," he said. "I always come home," and nudged in closer to me.

"Don't get me wrong, I'm happy to see you, but where have you been?"

"I just had to get out of town for a bit."

"For a bit?" I said. "It's been weeks."

"I had to sort some things out, but I don't want to get into it."

"How long are you going to be here?"

"Geez, what's with the questions? Can't you just be happy to see me?" He pulled me closer and pressed himself against me.

"You've gained a little weight," he said, grinning. I moved away a little.

"I like it," he said, his hands roving my belly and hips, kissing me. "You're not..." he stopped kissing me and looked into my eyes.

"What?" I said.

"Pregnant?"

I just looked at him and nodded slightly.

"You're pregnant? Are you sure? You're not just late?"

I pulled down my shirt, rolled away from him and retrieved the little ultrasound shot the technician had given me. "Here," I said, handing it to him.

He looked at me in disbelief, slowly taking the image from me. "This, in here," he said, looking down at my belly. "No shit. Not this too. I don't need this." He put his head in his hands. "But it's kinda cool. Are you gonna ask me to marry you now?" he said, looking at me with his big green, sometimes hazel, sometimes grey eyes.

"I'll be all right," I said, "on my own."

"So you don't wanna marry me."

"I never know whether you're coming or going. That doesn't work for me."

"But you're happy to see me now."

"Yes, I'm happy to see you!" I said. "I'm happy you're ok, you're in one piece and you're here. But you'll leave again, too, of that I'm sure."

"Don't put words in my mouth."

"Look," I said, "we didn't plan this. It happened and here we are."

"You know, I had a feeling."

"You did? Is that why you came back?"

"That and, I don't know. I didn't feel great about the way I left, but I didn't want to get you involved. Anyway, you're sure?"

I held out the image to him once more. He shook his head. "Let's forget about it for a moment. Come here," he said and kissed me for a long, long time, slow and deep. I melted into him.

"Hmmmm," he said, when we finally opened our eyes and just held each other. "I've missed this."

"Me too," I said. "It's been too long."

"Why don't you come with me?" he said.

"To?"

"Just come with me. We'll go north. Maybe work for the Hudson's Bay Company way up north. Work like crazy, make lots of money."

"You mean, like in the Northwest Territories? That far north?"

"Yeah, I was talkin' to someone the other day who did just that. Him and his wife decided to do that for a year. I mean, there's nothin' to spend your money on, apart from whatever you need and you could get that from the HBC. And then just save. You even get a special allowance for working up north."

"You've really thought about this?" I said. "I've never heard you speak about something with so much enthusiasm."

"It just seems like the perfect solution," he said.

I took a deep breath.

"What?" he said.

"Have you settled up with Big Steve?" I asked, hesitantly. "All that money you owed him?"

"What do you think I've been doing?

"I don't know," I said. "All I know is that you disappeared without a trace and then one day, I get a package in the mail with these beautifully carved spoons, no return address and here you are. That's what I know."

"Those spoons are pretty cool, eh? I thought you could

use some decent salad utensils. It took me hundreds of hours to carve them."

"They're gorgeous," I said.

"I thought about you a lot while I was away," he said.

"Oh yeah?"

"Yeah, sometimes I thought how your eyes would light up when you saw these spoons and then other times I thought, why am I doing this?"

"Why would you say something like that?" I said, pulling away from him.

He shrugged.

"I don't know. Just being a jerk, I guess. I'm sorry. I was just looking forward to seeing you, to spending a couple of days with you. This news has thrown me for a loop."

"I know. It's thrown me as well," I said. "So, what are your plans now?"

"Dunno. Have you told your family?" he asked.

"No," I said. "Only Annie. No one else. I wish it was just you and me," I added quietly.

"What was that?" he said.

"I said I wish it was just you and me and not my family and not Big Steve and money issues and all that."

"It would be just the two of us if we went up north."

"Yeah, but it just doesn't seem very realistic," I said, my heart pounding. "I really don't want you to go, but I know you don't want to be here, not really." My eyes welled up with tears. I swallowed hard. "I love you. And I'm scared for you. And worried."

"I can take care of myself," he said, putting his arms around me, holding me. "Don't worry about me." He held me closer, kissing the top of my head. "I love you, too."

With one arm still around my waist, he reached into his jeans pocket and pulled out the small, jagged piece of jade I had given him, what seemed like years ago now. He had started working with it, following the natural lines of the stone, waiting for an image to reveal itself.

"I told you once that when we broke up, I would return this to you."

I looked at it, my eyes blurred with tears. I held it in my hand for a few minutes, turning it over and over. "I want you to keep it," I said. "Make something beautiful." I held it out to him. He took it and held my hand for a moment.

"It's pretty hard to work with. See the marks on it? I tried to do something with it, but I gave up."

"I'm sure you'll find a way," I said, smiling.

About Atmosphere Press

Atmosphere Press is an independent, full-service publisher for excellent books in all genres and for all audiences. Learn more about what we do at atmospherepress.com.

We encourage you to check out some of Atmosphere's latest releases, which are available at Amazon.com and via order from your local bookstore:

For a Better Life, a novel by Julia Reid Galosy

Tales of Little Egypt, a historical novel by James Gilbert

The Hidden Life, a novel by Robert Castle

Big Beasts, a novel by Patrick Scott

Alvarado, a novel by John W. Horton III

Nothing to Get Nostalgic About, a novel by Eddie Brophy

GROW: A Jack and Lake Creek Book, a novel by Chris S McGee

Home is Not This Body, a novel by Karahn Washington

Whose Mary Kate, a novel by Jane Leclere Doyle

Stuck and Drunk in Shadyside, young adult fiction by M. Byerly

These Things Happen, a novel by Chris Caldwell

Vanity: Murder in the Name of Sin, a novel by Rhiannon Garrard

Blood of the True Believer, a novel by Brandann R. Hill-Mann

About the Author

Betty R. Wall was born and raised in British Columbia, Canada. From a young age, Betty has had a love of language and the written word, which ultimately led her to pursue a

Photo by Cloe I. Logan

degree in Germanic Languages and Literatures at the University of Toronto. For most of her professional career, she has owned and operated a translation and interpretation agency. Alongside this profession, a keen interest in creative writing took her to Barbara Turner-Vesselago's Freefall Writing workshops in various parts of the world. *No Way Out* had its beginnings in one such workshop. This is her first novella.

CPSIA information can be obtained
at www.ICGtesting.com
Printed in the USA
BVHW080437161020
591156BV00001B/91